D0611540

SUN & MOON

Play Ball, Pikachu!

Adapted by Sonia Sander

ISBN 978-1-338-23752-8

10 9 8 7 6 5 4 3 2 1 18 19 20 21 22

Printed in the U.S.A. 40

First printing 2018

Book design by Carolyn Bull

SCHOLASTIC INC.

Ash was watching TV with his Pokémon Pikachu and Rockruff. It was the last Pokémon Base game of the season.

"Awesome!" Ash cheered. "This game is getting so good!"

It was almost the end of the game.
The team's star, Oluolu, hit a home run.
The Magikarp team won!
"So cool!" Ash said. "I want to play Pokémon Base, too."

The next day at Pokémon School, Ash got his wish.

"Today's class is all about Pokémon Base," Professo Kukui said.

"Are you going to teach us?" Lana asked.

"Not me," said Professor Kukui. "I asked a great coach to do that."

"It's Oluolu!" Ash cried.

"And who's that behind him?!" Lillie wondered.

It was his Pokémon partner, Snorlax!

The enormous Pokémon squeezed into the room and fell asleep.

Oluolu taught the class all about Pokémon Base.
They split into two teams and got ready to play.
Rotom Dex called the game.
“First to take the field is Team Kiawe!”

Kiawe took the pitcher's mound.
Ash came up to bat.
"Here it comes, Ash," Kiawe warned.
"Bring it on!" Ash yelled back.

Kiawe wound his arm back.
Bright flames burst all around him.
“Inferno Overdrive Ball!” Kiawe cried.
The ball blasted toward Ash.

“Look out!” Ash called. “Gigavolt Havoc Swing!”
Ash swung with all his might.
But he missed.

"You've got to keep your eye on the ball!" Sophocles told Ash.

"I know, I know," Ash said.

He tried again and again to hit the ball.

But Ash missed them all. He struck out.

It was Kiawe's turn at bat.

Pikachu was on the mound.

"Pikachu," Ash called. "Show them some of that pepper, buddy."

"Give me your best shot," Kiawe replied. "Whatever it is, it's gone!"

Pikachu spun the ball and threw hard.
The ball screamed toward home plate.
Kiawe hit the ball high in the air.
"Say it's not so!" Kiawe cried. "A pop-up?!"

The ball flew toward Sophocles.
He tripped over his feet and fell.
But he still caught the ball!
Team Ash went on to win the game!

Ash was thrilled, until he saw Jessie, James, and Meowth had arrived!

"Team Rocket? What are you doing here?!" Kiawe demanded.

"I want Oluolu's autograph," Jessie gushed.

Ash and his friends knew Team Rocket was up to no good. Soon they were all arguing.

"Why don't we settle this with a game? I will give my autograph to the winning team," Oluolu said. "Snorlax and I will play on Team School."

James was worried about playing against Oluolu. But Jessie pointed out that Snorlax was on the field. The Sleeping Pokémon was already yawning.

"Don't worry," Jessie said. "Just hit the ball to Snorlax."

Pikachu's pitch made Jessie spin.

But she still hit the ball right at Snorlax.

It bounced off Snorlax's tummy and rolled across the field.

Kiawe grabbed the ball, but Snorlax rolled on top of him!

"I win! I win!" Jessie cried.
But she forgot which way to run.
Rockruff tagged Jessie out.
"You bragged, now you are TAGGED!" Meowth yelled

James hit the ball right at Snorlax, too.

Oluolu ran in to catch the ball. He tried to get Snorlax to stand up.

"Wake up! I can't do this on my own!" he cried.

But Snorlax just kept sleeping.

Now it was Team School's turn at bat.
Mimikyu took the mound.
Pikachu headed to home plate to bat for Team School.
"We're counting on you, Pikachu!" Ash cheered.

“I’ve never seen Mimikyu so charged up,” Meowth cried.

Mimikyu glowed an electric purple.

It fired a foul ball right at Pikachu!

Pikachu got up and brushed off the dirt.
Ash made sure Pikachu was okay.
"Hey, that's against the rules!" he shouted.
Jessie got the message. She sent in a new pitcher.

It was Meowth!

He struck out Kiawe.

Team School was having a hard time hitting Team Rocket's pitches.

The game was down to the last inning.

Oluolu stepped up to the plate.

"As long as I'm on the mound, you're outbound," Meowth bragged.

But Oluolu smashed the ball past Meowth.

Now Snorlax was at bat. It yawned as it stepped up to the plate.

"Yay, Snorlax!" Lana called.

"Give us a home run," Ash added.

Meowth threw a curveball at Snorlax.
Snorlax didn't move.
The ball bounced off its bat and onto the ground.

The ball bounced right to Team Rocket's Mareanie.
"Grab that, Mareanie!" Meowth called.
Mareanie stabbed the ball with its horn.

"Over here!" James called.

Mareanie blasted off the ground and flew across the field.

It landed right on James's face!

The ball dropped to the ground!

Oluolu ran home. Now the score was tied!
Meowth ran for the loose ball.
It was all up to Snorlax. But it didn't move.
"Snorlax, run!" Ash cried.

Oluolu stepped in and raised his Z-Ring.

"Now it's time to pull out all the stops. Passion! And sweat! Tears and guts! Feel the burn! Run, Snorlax! Use Pulverizing Pancake, go!"

Suddenly, Snorlax was unstoppable!
It raced around the bases.
Meowth threw the ball home to Wobbuffet.
But Snorlax flattened Wobbuffet like a pancake.

"Safe!" called Professor Kukui.

Team School had done it. They had won the Pokémon Base game!

Our heroes celebrated their victory!